Candy Kingdom Chaos

Nancy Drew
CLUE BOOK

#7

Candy Kingdom Chaos

BY CAROLYN KEENE * ILLUSTRATED BY PETER FRANCIS

Aladdin
NEW YORK   LONDON   TORONTO   SYDNEY   NEW DELHI

This book is a work of fiction. Any references to historical events, real people, or real places are used fictitiously. Other names, characters, places, and events are products of the author's imagination, and any resemblance to actual events or places or persons, living or dead, is entirely coincidental.

ALADDIN

An imprint of Simon & Schuster Children's Publishing Division
1230 Avenue of the Americas, New York, New York 10020
First Aladdin paperback edition March 2017
Text copyright © 2017 by Simon & Schuster, Inc.
Illustrations copyright © 2017 by Peter Francis
Also available in an Aladdin hardcover edition.
ALADDIN and related logo are registered trademarks of Simon & Schuster, Inc.
NANCY DREW, NANCY DREW CLUE BOOK, and colophons
are registered trademarks of Simon & Schuster, Inc.
All rights reserved, including the right of reproduction in whole or in part in any form.
For information about special discounts for bulk purchases, please contact
Simon & Schuster Special Sales at 1-866-506-1949 or business@simonandschuster.com.
The Simon & Schuster Speakers Bureau can bring authors to your live event.
For more information or to book an event contact the Simon & Schuster Speakers Bureau
at 1-866-248-3049 or visit our website at www.simonspeakers.com.
Designed by Karina Granda
The illustrations for this book were rendered digitally.
The text of this book was set in Adobe Garamond Pro.
Manufactured in the United States of America 0217 OFF
2 4 6 8 10 9 7 5 3 1
Library of Congress Control Number 2016961755
ISBN 978-1-4814-5827-6 (hc)
ISBN 978-1-4814-5826-9 (pbk)
ISBN 978-1-4814-5828-3 (eBook)

* CONTENTS *

Chapter

1

SWEET SUCCESS

"Spring break—here we come!" eight-year-old Nancy Drew cheered to her two best friends.

George Fayne's dark curls bounced as she nodded her head. "You mean Candy Kingdom here we come," she pointed out. "If we're lucky."

"I won't be lucky." Bess Marvin sighed. "I forgot to wear my lucky purple socks."

Nancy thought they were all lucky to be at the mall that Friday afternoon. It was the last day of school before spring break. It seemed like every kid in River Heights was there for the Candy Kingdom contest.

Candy Kingdom was a new amusement park opening in River Heights the next day. It would have candy-style rides and candy games—even candy characters, like the superfamous Sour Power Pals!

"Remind me what the rules of the contest are," Bess said, twirling a lock of her blond hair. "Not that I'll win."

"Anyone can win, Bess," Nancy said with an assuring smile. "All you have to do is pick the chocolate bar with the gold crown inside."

"If you do," George went on, "you win four passes to Candy Kingdom to use every day during spring break."

"And that means riding the Twisting Taffy Coaster every single day," Nancy reminded them. "I heard that it flips upside down!"

"The coaster or our stomachs?" George joked.

The girls turned their faces toward the stage set up in the atrium that day.

"I heard there's going to be a dance show before

the chocolate-bar contest," Nancy said. "Nadine told me she's one of the dancers."

Bess and George weren't surprised. Nadine Nardo was the class actress, dancer, singer—and sometimes drama queen!

As the mall filled up with more kids, Nancy felt someone tap her shoulder. Turning, she saw Andrea Wu, another classmate. If Nadine was the class actress, Andrea was the class candy lover—and proud of it.

"Hi, Andrea," Nancy said with a wave.

Andrea said hi back. She then looked from Nancy to Bess to George and said, "If one of you wins, will you take the other two to Candy Kingdom?"

"For sure," Nancy confirmed. "We're a team."

"Even when we're not solving mysteries," Bess added.

Everyone at River Heights Elementary School knew that Nancy, Bess, and George were the Clue Crew, detectives who solved mysteries at school and all over town. Nancy was proud of all the mysteries they had solved so far. She was also proud of her Clue Book where she wrote down all their suspects, clues, and thoughts.

"So if one of you wins . . . ," Andrea said slowly. "Four minus three . . . equals one."

"So?" George asked.

"So that leaves one more Candy Kingdom pass for another friend," Andrea said with a grin. "Like me! And you know how much I love candy. See my earrings made out of real jelly beans?" Andrea tugged her earlobes.

"Pretty!" Nancy told Andrea. "But we really haven't figured out who we'd take yet."

"Take *me*!" Andrea stated. "I invited you to my birthday party at the Sugar Sweet Spa a few weeks ago. Remember the candy-scented manicures? And the hot-cocoa foot soaks?"

"How could I forget?" George groaned. "I've been digging marshmallows out from between my toes ever since."

Nancy was about to ask Andrea who she would take to Candy Kingdom if she won, until—

"*Eek!*" Andrea cried.

Someone had dangled a wiggly spider in front of Andrea's face. When Nancy, Bess, and George heard a familiar snicker, they knew who it was.

"Antonio Elefano!" Bess snapped angrily as their grinning classmate stepped out from behind Andrea.

If Nadine was the class actress and Andrea was the class candy lover, Antonio was the class pest.

"It's just one of my Gummy Pests candies." Antonio laughed as he bit a squiggly, wiggly leg off the spider. "My favorite candy."

"It takes a pest to eat one!" Andrea snapped as she huffed away.

Nancy, Bess, and George wanted to move away from Antonio too, but an excited roar suddenly filled the mall. It was Mayor Strong being led onto the stage by two Sour Power Pals!

Besides the candy, the Sour Power Pals had their own cartoon TV show. On it they acted as sour as they tasted.

"I don't think I like those Sour Power Pals," Bess said with a frown. "They think they're so smart."

"You mean tart," George joked.

The microphone screeched before Mayor Strong announced, "Welcome to the Candy Kingdom Contest. But before we bring out the king and queen of Candy Kingdom, let's raise the roof for the Tippy-Toe Tappers of River Heights!"

"There's Nadine!" Nancy shouted as a half dozen kids in candy costumes tapped to the middle of the stage with their arms looped together.

Nadine wore a green leotard with a matching giant gumdrop on her head. Smiling, she tapped her dancing feet to the tune "I Want Candy."

Nancy, Bess, and George danced to the beat—until something horrible happened. Nadine's giant green gumdrop tipped forward and covered her eyes! With both of her arms still looped, her hands weren't free to push the gumdrop back up.

"Oh no!" Nancy gasped. "How will Nadine dance with a gumdrop over her face?"

"Like a klutz!" George groaned.

But to everyone's surprise Nadine kept dancing in perfect step with the others. After the music ended, she even took the perfect bow!

"Nadine nailed it!" George cheered.

Nancy was proud of Nadine. She was so proud that she had an idea. "If one of us wins," she told Bess and George, "let's give Nadine our fourth pass to Candy Kingdom."

"Good idea," George agreed. "After what she just went through, she deserves a break."

"And we deserve a break from Antonio Elefano!" Bess complained as she brushed another Gummy Pest from her face.

The Tippy-Toe Tappers were replaced onstage by the king and queen of Candy Kingdom. Instead of jewels, their crowns and scepters were adorned with colorful candies.

"Kids of the kingdom!" the king boomed. "The Sour Power Pals stand before you to hand out chocolate bars. You are to take one each."

"But do not open them until I give the royal thumbs-up," the queen added.

Carrying big bags of chocolate bars, the Sour Power Pals made their way through the crowd. Nancy, Bess, and George each took one bar.

Antonio grabbed one too. When he read the label, he scowled and shouted, "This chocolate bar has coconut inside. I hate coconut!"

But when Antonio reached to switch bars, the purple Sour Power Pal yanked away the bag. "No exchanges, kid," he said. "Deal with it."

Antonio refused to deal with it. Antonio turned to Bess and said, "Swap with me. Give me your chocolate-peanut bar for my chocolate coconut."

"What difference does it make what flavor it is?" Bess asked. "What's important is if it has a gold crown inside."

"I'm going to eat it whether I win or lose," Antonio said. "Will you swap with me or not?"

Bess narrowed her eyes at Antonio. "If we swap, will you go away and leave us alone?" she asked.

"Sure," Antonio insisted.

"Deal," Bess said as she made the switch.

"Bess, what were you thinking?" George asked as Antonio squeezed through the crowd away from the girls.

"What if you gave Antonio the winning

chocolate bar?" Nancy wanted to know.

"It can't be the winning bar," Bess said. "I forgot to wear my lucky purple socks, remember?"

After everyone had a chocolate bar, the queen called out, "Kids of the kingdom, I command you all to open your chocolate bars now!"

Nancy scrambled to tear off the wrapping of her chocolate-marshmallow bar. She frowned when she found no gold crown inside. George's chocolate-raisin bar was crown-free too. But when Bess tore open hers, she let out a gigantic squeal.

"I got it! I got it!" Bess cried, waving a tiny crown-shaped paper high in the air. "I got the gold crown!"

Nancy and George were about to cheer too. Until someone reached over Bess's shoulder and snatched the gold crown right out of her hand!

Chapter

SNIDE RIDE

"My crown!" Bess cried, glancing around in a panic. "Who took my winning crown?"

Nancy wasn't surprised to see Antonio standing behind Bess with the crown in his hand.

"You mean *my* crown," Antonio said. "The winning chocolate-coconut bar was mine and you know it."

"It was," Nancy told Antonio, "until you swapped it with Bess!"

"Blah, blah, blah." Antonio sighed.

"Nancy, George," Bess wailed, "do something!"

Mayor Strong shaded his eyes from the lights as he gazed into the audience. "Do we have a winner?" he called out. "Will the lucky winner with the gold crown please step up?"

Antonio was about to run toward the stage when—

"Wait, Antonio," George said, pointing down at his feet. "Your sneaker lace is untied."

"Huh?" Antonio said.

The moment Antonio glanced down, George grabbed the crown and handed it to Bess. The three friends then pushed their way through the crowd and to the stage.

"Hey, no fair!" Antonio yelled after them. "You could at least give me your fourth pass to Candy Kingdom!"

Antonio's angry voice trailed off as Nancy, Bess, and George raced onto the stage. Polite cheers and disappointed groans erupted as Bess waved the gold crown.

"We have our winner!" the king announced.

He smiled at Nancy and George. "And these must be her lucky friends."

Mayor Strong held the mike as Nancy, Bess, and George introduced themselves. The queen then handed them three red-and-white candy-striped bracelets to snap around their wrists.

Nancy brushed her reddish-blond bangs aside and admired her prize bracelet. It was made of rubber, but it was as precious as gold. With it, she, Bess, and George would get into Candy Kingdom for a whole week—for free!

"Well done," the queen declared, "but who will wear the fourth bracelet?"

Bess stepped up to the mike and said, "She's the gumdrop dancer with the wardrobe malfunction—meet Nadine Nardo!"

A shrieking Nadine scurried across the stage, her shoes tapping and her gumdrop hat in place. "Thanks, you guys!" she said excitedly. "Thank yoooooooou!!!"

The queen handed Nadine the fourth bracelet. "Congratulations, Lady Gumdrop," she praised heartily.

As the four friends took a bow, they spotted Andrea at the foot of the stage. Andrea glared angrily at Nancy, Bess, and George before storming off.

"Why is Andrea so mad?" Bess whispered. "It's not like we promised her the fourth bracelet."

"Andrea is mad, all right," George agreed. "But check out how happy Nadine is."

Nancy turned to see Nadine smiling from ear to ear. Other gumdrops had crowded around to congratulate her.

"Nadine is superhappy," Nancy agreed, "and this time she's not acting!"

"Who's excited about Candy Kingdom?" Hannah Gruen asked as she drove the girls to the amusement park the next morning.

Hannah had been the Drew's housekeeper since Nancy was only three years old. Like a mother, Hannah gave Nancy lots of hugs. She also gave Nancy lots of advice, like to do her homework, keep her room clean, and not eat too much candy at Candy Kingdom!

"We all are, Hannah!" Nancy declared.

"Especially me," Nadine said. She raised her wrist. "Getting this bracelet is as awesome as getting the lead in the class play."

"And you always do!" Bess praised.

Hannah parked the car at Candy Kingdom. They then walked the short distance to the gate. All four girls wore light spring jackets for the first mild day of the season. Nadine's jacket had three-quarter sleeves to show off her prize bracelet.

At the gate a woman whose name tag read CHERYL checked the girls' bracelets. She also made sure they were snapped on tightly.

"Congratulations, winners," Cheryl told them. "Remember not to take your bracelets off while . you're in the park."

"I'm not taking it off all week," George declared.

"Since when do you change your outfits anyway, George?" Bess teased.

George rolled her eyes at Bess. The two were cousins but different in every way. Bess was fashion-forward, loving the latest styles and accessories. George was fashion-backward, but she didn't care as long as her accessories included the latest electronics.

While Hannah got her guest bracelet, the four friends looked through the candy-decorated gate. The park had opened an hour ago, but it was already packed with kids rushing to the rides and games.

"Check it out!" George said, pointing through

the gate. "There's the Twisting Taffy Coaster."

"Twisting Taffy Coaster?" Nadine repeated as they gazed at the extreme coaster with the twisting loops. "Does it go upside down?"

"That's the best part!" someone with a familiar voice said.

Andrea was standing right behind them. Nancy was surprised to see her smiling.

"My mom bought me a ticket for Candy Kingdom," Andrea told the girls excitedly. "I can't go all week, but I can be here all day."

Then using both of her hands, Andrea shook Nadine's hand. "Congratulations, Nadine. You deserve the fourth bracelet." Still smiling, Andrea walked away.

"I guess she's not mad anymore," Nancy decided.

When Hannah returned, it was all systems go! "Okay, girls," Hannah said as they walked through the gate, "what would you like to do first?"

"That!" Bess said, pointing to a candy-striped game booth. The game was called Ring the Peppermint Sticks. Red-and-white-striped pepper-mint sticks stood straight up in a row as kids aimed to toss rings over them.

"The peppermints match our bracelets!" Bess said.

"Is that the only reason you want to play?" George groaned. "Let's ride the Twisting Taffy Coaster first."

"George is right," Nancy told Bess. "We wanted to ride the Twisting Taffy Coaster—"

"No!" Nadine cut in. "Let's ride *that* first!"

Nancy, Bess, and George looked to see where Nadine was pointing. A few feet away was a boat ride called the World of the Sour Power Pals.

"The Sour Power Pals ride?" Nancy asked.

"But the line for the Twisting Taffy Coaster is getting long, Nadine," George said.

"I don't care!" Nadine exclaimed. "I want to ride the Sour Power Pals ride—and I want to ride it now!" Nadine spun dramatically on her heel. She then began running straight for the boats.

"Great," George groaned. "We had to give our fourth bracelet to a drama queen."

Hannah promised to meet the girls at the same spot after the ride. Nancy, Bess, and George joined Nadine where Sour Power Pals were helping kids into boats.

When the blue pal saw the girls and their candy-striped bracelets, he sneered, "Well! It looks like we've got the contest winners!"

"Oh yeah?" the yellow pal said. "Even winners enter our ride at their own risk."

"Risk?" Bess gasped.

"That's right," the red pal sneered. "Anything can happen in there—anything rotten!"

As they approached the boat, Nancy told Bess, "They're just pretending to be sour—just like their candy."

"Well, I prefer sweet!" Bess insisted.

Nancy was the last to climb into the boat. As she waited her turn, she overheard one Sour Power Pal ask another: "Are those prize bracelets valuable or what?"

"For sure," another pal replied. "Any one of

my friends would want that bracelet for a free week at Candy Kingdom."

Nancy was about to glance back at the pals when George shouted, "Hurry up, Nancy. Before you miss the boat!"

"Coming!" Nancy called as she quickly embarked.

Bess and George sat in the first seat, and Nancy and Nadine sat in the second. The boat rocked as more kids climbed into the third seat, but none of the girls turned around to look to see who they were. All eyes were on the tunnel leading into the ride.

Was it as scary as the Sour Power Pals said it would be? They would soon find out!

A bell clanged and the boat floated down a green syrupy stream. Nancy drew in her breath as it slipped beneath a candy-decorated arch into a dark world smelling like sour candies!

"Cool!" George gasped.

As the boat sloshed downstream the girls were surprised by Sour Power Pals all around, jumping out to sing the theme song of their show: "Who needs sweet when you can be sour? And we're more sour by the hour!"

The ride was more fun than scary. All four girls shrieked happily as the boat came within inches of being blasted with powdered sugar. They shrieked even louder when the boat dipped into a pink-and-blue cotton-candy vat whirling around and around!

Further down the stream, two more Sour Power Pals perched on a rock-candy mountain bounced marshmallows off their boat.

The boat approached another arch. This one had the words BON-BON VOYAGE painted over it. Sitting on top of the arch was another pal aiming a camera down at the boat.

"Say 'Cheesy!'" the pal shouted before taking a flash picture.

Nancy blinked as they floated from the dark ride into bright sunshine. After climbing out of the boat, the four friends traded high fives.

"That was awesome," Nadine admitted.

"Aren't you glad I made you go on it?"

"Totally," Nancy agreed. "Now let's ride the Twisting Taffy Coaster."

"Last one to the Twisting Taffy Coaster is a rotten marshmallow!" George shouted.

Nancy called to Hannah where they were going next. She, Bess, and George began running toward the Twisting Taffy Coaster when Nadine shouted, "You guys—stop!!!"

The girls did stop. They turned to see Nadine standing wide-eyed and statue-still.

"What's wrong, Nadine?" Nancy called.

Nadine lifted her arm and cried, "My candy-striped bracelet. It's gone!"

Chapter

CANDY-STRIPE SWIPE

"Gone?" Nancy gasped.

"What do you mean it's gone?" George asked.

The girls crowded around Nadine's arm. The candy-striped bracelet that had dangled around her wrist was no longer there.

"I just noticed it was gone," Nadine cried. "I must have lost it inside the Sour Power Pals ride."

"No problem then," Nancy said with a smile. "We'll find someone in charge of the ride to look for it—"

"No!" Nadine cut in. "They'll stop the ride, and everyone will hate me."

Nancy and Bess tried to calm Nadine, but George didn't get it. "How could the bracelet fall off your wrist when it was double-snapped?" she asked.

"Somewhere in the middle of the ride I felt a tug," Nadine said, her eyes wide. "Maybe the bracelet got caught on something."

"Did you see what it got caught on?" Bess asked.

"How could I?" Nadine cried. "It was dark inside!"

Nancy didn't know what to do. Without the bracelet Nadine wouldn't get into Candy Kingdom every day for free.

"It's my fault for not being careful!" Nadine exclaimed, blinking back tears. "I'm not having fun anymore."

Hannah seemed to guess something was wrong. She hurried over and asked, "What's the problem, girls?"

"Everything!" Nadine cried. "I want to go home."

"But we just got here!" George groaned.

Hannah placed a gentle hand on Nadine's shoulder. "There's no reason to stay if you're upset," she said. "I'll drive you home."

"Should we go too?" Nancy asked.

"No!" Nadine blurted. "If you leave Candy Kingdom because of me, then you'll hate me too!"

Hannah wasn't sure about leaving the girls at Candy Kingdom, but they promised to stick together at all times.

"Don't leave the park," Hannah reminded the girls. "And I'll meet you back at the Sour Power Pals ride in an hour."

Nadine mumbled good-bye and then walked away sadly with Hannah.

"Poor Nadine." Bess sighed.

"I'd be upset too if I lost my bracelet," George

agreed. "But I still don't get how it just fell off."

Nancy didn't get it either. Their bracelets were snapped on so tightly. Then she had a thought: What if someone inside the ride pulled Nadine's bracelet off? Someone like the Sour Power Pal that Nancy overheard?

"Nadine said she felt a tug on her wrist," Nancy remembered. "As if something pulled it off."

"So?" George asked.

"So maybe it wasn't *something* that pulled off her bracelet," Nancy went on. "Maybe it was *someone*."

"Someone stole the bracelet?" Bess gasped.

"It wasn't just any bracelet," Nancy pointed out. "It was a free ticket to Candy Kingdom for a whole week."

"Hmmm," George said with a sly smile. "Something tells me the Clue Crew has a brand-new case."

"Here?" Bess asked. "At Candy Kingdom?"

"Mysteries can happen anywhere!" Nancy said. She reached into her jacket pocket and pulled out her Clue Book. "Come on, Clue Crew. Let's get to work!"

Nancy, Bess, and George sat down on an empty bench facing the Caramel Carousel. It looked just like a giant sundae with caramel topping. Even the carousel horses were caramel-colored with chocolate-colored manes and tails.

Nancy opened her Clue Book to a clean page. Using her favorite pencil topped with a cupcake eraser, she wrote the word "Suspects" on a new page. A few lines under that she wrote: "Sour Power Pals."

"Sour Power Pals?" George asked.

"Why would the pals want a free week at Candy Kingdom?" Bess asked. "They work there every day."

"I heard the pals talking," Nancy explained. "One said that any of his friends would love a free week at Candy Kingdom."

"We saw lots of Sour Power Pals inside the ride too," Bess recalled. "That's where Nadine said she lost the bracelet."

"Those pals are bad news on their TV show," George said with a shrug. "They could be bad news in real life, too."

"Maybe," Nancy agreed. "And until we find out more, the Sour Power Pals are our first suspects."

Nancy looked up from her Clue Book, wondering who else could have taken Nadine's bracelet. Watching the carousel spin, Nancy saw someone she knew ride by on a caramel-colored horse. It was Andrea!

"Andrea is on the carousel," Nancy told Bess and George. "Let's wave hi when she comes around again."

Nancy, Bess, and George stood up to wait as the carousel turned. After a few more seconds Andrea's horse came around the bend, but as she got closer Nancy noticed something else. Something familiar!

"Andrea's wearing a bracelet!" Nancy exclaimed. "A red-and-white bracelet!"

Chapter

BRACELET CHASE-LET

"Are you sure, Nancy?" George asked.

"See for yourself," Nancy said as they waited for Andrea's carousel horse to come around again. This time they all saw Andrea's bracelet. It was red and white, just like theirs!

"I couldn't see if it was striped," Nancy said.

"Red and white is close enough," George said as Andrea's horse turned out of sight. "But how could Andrea have gotten the missing bracelet?"

"We didn't see her inside the Sour Power Pals ride," Bess said.

"But we did see Andrea before the ride," Nancy pointed out, "when she shook Nadine's hand." After placing her Clue Book on the bench, she showed them. "Andrea used both hands to shake." She grabbed Bess's hand. "One of Andrea's hands might have covered Nadine's wrist while the other hand pulled off her bracelet."

"I get it," George said.

"So do I," Bess said with a small smile. "Now can I have my hand back?"

The carousel slowed down. Nancy scribbled Andrea's name on her suspect list. Next to Andrea's name she added the words "double handshake."

"I hope Andrea didn't take Nadine's bracelet." Bess sighed. "She's our friend."

"I know," Nancy agreed. "But my dad says even friends make mistakes sometimes."

The carousel came to a complete stop. While kids climbed off the caramel-colored horses, the girls looked for Andrea. They saw her walking away from the carousel.

After saying something to her mother, Andrea began running in the opposite direction. Nancy, Bess, and George ran too—after Andrea!

"Andrea, wait!" Nancy shouted.

Andrea stopped and turned around. When she saw the girls, she called, "I told my mom I'd be right back. What do you want?"

"We want that bracelet you're wearing!" George shouted. "That's what!"

Andrea stared at the bracelet on her wrist. She then shook her head and said, "No way! This bracelet is mine!" Andrea raced off again—this time to what looked like a forest of giant colorful lollipops. A sign next to the entrance read LOLLI-POP LABYRINTH.

"What's a *lab-er-inth*?" Bess asked after Andrea darted straight into it.

"There's only way to find out," George said. "We're going in!"

Nancy, Bess, and George slipped under the

arch-entrance. They froze when they found themselves between rows and rows of giant lollipops.
Between the rows was a maze of paths leading in
all different directions!

"Where did Andrea go?" Nancy wondered.

"I have a better question," Bess said, looking
around. "Where do we go?"

The girls flitted down different paths, but not
one led to Andrea. They just led to more giant
lollipops!

"I don't care about finding Andrea anymore!"
Bess wailed. "I just want to get out of here!"

Nancy watched as more kids got lost inside

the Lollipop Labyrinth. She wanted to get out too. But how?

"Peter Patino had a hamster maze at the science fair," George told Nancy and Bess. "His hamster, Nibbles, sniffed his way out to food at the other end."

"We're not hamsters," Nancy argued. "We're humans."

"True," George said. "But my human nose smells cheese popcorn."

Nancy, Bess, and George followed their noses through the Lollipop Labyrinth until the strong cheesy smell led them outside. Standing nearby were snack booths called the Sugar Shacks. A sign on one booth read CORNY-POP.

"We found the popcorn." Nancy sighed. "But we didn't find Andrea."

"What do you mean?" Bess said, pointing. "There she is buying cotton candy!"

The Clue Crew crept up behind Andrea at the cotton-candy stand. Her back was to the girls as she paid for a cone of pink-and-blue cotton candy.

Nancy nodded toward Andrea's outstretched arm. Dangling from her wrist was a red-and-white bracelet. A red-and-white *candy-striped* bracelet—just like Nadine's!

"Andrea?" George blurted as she tapped Andrea's shoulder.

"Huh?" Andrea spun around with surprise, ramming a wad of cotton candy in George's face!

"Yuck-o!" George cried. "You got cotton candy in my face, Andrea!"

"And you got your face in my cotton candy—*Georgia*!" Andrea complained.

George glowered at the sound of her real name.

As George pulled sticky strands off of her cheek and chin, Nancy pointed to Andrea's bracelet. "Let us see that, Andrea," Nancy urged.

"Please?" Bess added.

"As if that's ever going to happen," Andrea snapped. "Leave me alone!"

As Andrea pulled her hand all the way back, the bracelet flew off her wrist. It hovered in the air before dropping to the ground with a loud *CLUNK*!

George pointed to the bracelet as it began rolling away. "What are we waiting for?" she cried. "Let's get it."

"Let's not," Nancy said.

"Nancy, why not?" Bess asked.

"Because," Nancy replied, "I don't think that's Nadine's missing bracelet."

Chapter

GUEST PEST

"What do you mean it's not the missing bracelet, Nancy?" George asked.

"Our bracelets are rubber," Nancy explained. "And rubber doesn't clunk."

"Nancy's right," Bess agreed. "It's more like a boing. Then it bounces."

Nancy picked up the bracelet and handed it to Andrea. "I'm sorry, Andrea," she said. "This really is yours."

"I told you it was!" Andrea insisted. She picked

up the red-and-white bracelet and said, "I won it fair and square, okay?"

"Okay," Nancy agreed before Andrea hurried off.

"Are you sure that wasn't Nadine's bracelet?" George asked. "Where else would she get a candy-striped bracelet?"

Bess's eyes lit up. "Unless it wasn't a bracelet," she said.

"What do you mean?" Nancy asked.

"Andrea said she won it," Bess explained. "So come with me."

Bess led Nancy and George to the busy, noisy game booths. She pointed to the Ring the Peppermint Sticks and said, "The rings the kids are tossing are red and white and candy-striped."

Nancy, Bess, and George watched kids try their luck tossing rings around the peppermint sticks. Each ring made a loud *CLANG* as it dropped.

"Noisy much?" Bess asked with a smile. "Noisy like metal?"

"And Andrea's bracelet!" George declared.

"Good work, Bess," Nancy praised. "But if Andrea was wearing one of those rings—how did she get it?"

"Let's figure that out later," Bess said with a smile. "I want to play and win a stuffed purple unicorn!"

Bess stepped up to the booth where a teenage girl named Darcy handed her three metal rings to toss. Bess did her best tossing the rings, but they missed the peppermint sticks one by one.

"Bummer, Bess," George said.

"That's for sure." Bess sighed. "I really wanted that purple unicorn."

"But you do get something," Darcy said.

"I do?" Bess asked excitedly. "What?"

"You get one of the rings you tossed as a souvenir," Darcy replied, placing a ring on the ledge. "They make cool bracelets, you know."

Bess smiled and said, "Oh, we know!"

Nancy and George smiled. So that's how Andrea got her red-and-white candy-striped bracelet.

Bess thanked Darcy, but she left the metal ring on the ledge. They already had the best prize they could get from the game: a clue!

"We're pretty sure Andrea didn't take Nadine's bracelet," Nancy said as they walked away from the game booths. "Our only suspects left are the Sour Power Pals."

Just then two kids walked by. On their heads were twisted balloons shaped like bugs!

"Where did you get those?" George asked them.

"A guy is twisting balloons in the shape of Gummy Pests," the girl said excitedly.

"He just started if you want your own," the boy added.

As the kids walked away, Bess said, "I had enough of Gummy Pests yesterday, thanks to Antonio."

"At least Antonio isn't here today!" Nancy said.

The girls walked through Candy Kingdom until they reached the World of the Sour Power Pals. The same red, blue, and yellow pals from before were helping kids into boats. Nancy and George were about to approach them when Bess said, "Wait!"

"Now what?" George asked. "Don't tell me you want to play another game."

"No," Bess said, pointing to a nearby board covered with photos. "I want to see our picture from the Sour Power Pals ride!"

"Could we do that later, please?" Nancy asked Bess. "We should look for clues."

"I know, Nancy," Bess said, staring at the board. "But I think I just found one."

"What do you mean?" George asked.

Nancy and George joined Bess around the picture of them inside the boat. They could see who was sitting in the third seat. It was—

"Antonio Elefano!" Nancy exclaimed.

"With Tommy Maron from school," Bess pointed out. "They were right behind us, and we didn't even know it!"

"If Antonio was behind Nadine," Nancy said, "he could have reached over and taken her bracelet."

"Antonio was mad that I got the winning candy bar," Bess recalled, "and that we picked Nadine for Candy Kingdom instead of him."

"You know what this means," George said, narrowing her eyes at the picture. "Antonio Elefano is somewhere in Candy Kingdom today."

"He's also our next suspect," Nancy said as she wrote Antonio's name in her Clue Book. "And we have to find him!"

"Where, Nancy?" Bess asked. "Antonio and Tommy could be anywhere in Candy Kingdom!"

Nancy didn't know where to look first. But as she glanced up from her Clue Book, she spotted another kid with a twisted balloon on her head—a Gummy Pests balloon!

"Bess, George," Nancy said with a smile. "I think I know where to find Antonio."

Chapter

6

FERRIS SQUEAL

Nancy, Bess, and George looked around Candy Kingdom until they found the balloon-twister. A long line of kids wanting Gummy Pests balloons had already formed.

"There's Antonio and Tommy," George pointed out, "right in the middle of the line."

"I can't see if Antonio is wearing the bracelet," Bess said. "His sleeves are too long."

"Let's question him," Nancy suggested. She

knew Antonio would not cooperate, but they had to try!

"You again?" Antonio said when he saw the girls.

"You were in our boat on the Sour Power Pals ride," Nancy told him. "Weren't you?"

"You mean *you* were in *our* boat!" Antonio snapped.

"Yeah—our boat!" Tommy parroted.

"Who cares whose boat it was?" George argued. "Did you trick Nadine on it or what?"

"You bet I tricked her," Antonio boasted, "and the proof is in my pocket!"

Antonio patted his jacket pocket. Was Nadine's missing bracelet inside?

"Show us what's in your pocket, Antonio," Nancy said. Pointing to Antonio's pocket she took a small step forward.

Antonio took a giant step back. He then began shouting, "Hey! These girls are trying to jump the line!"

The kids behind them shouted too:

"Get at the end of the line!"

"Wait your turn!"

"We want Gummy Pests balloons too, you know!"

Nancy, Bess, and George didn't want Gummy Pests balloons. They wanted to know what was in Antonio's pocket.

"Antonio will never let us look in his pocket," Bess complained as the girls walked away from the line. "Not in a million years!"

The sound of happy shrieks suddenly filled the air. They were coming from the Flipping Fudge Pops Ferris Wheel, just a few feet away.

Nancy, Bess, and George smiled, watching the ride in action. Kids sat inside cages shaped like fudge pops. As the Ferris wheel turned—the cages flipped upside down!

"That gives me an idea!" George said with a grin.

Nancy and Bess followed George back to the balloon line. When Antonio saw the girls, he rolled his eyes.

"What do you want now?" Antonio asked.

"A challenge," George stated. She folded her arms across her chest. "We challenge you to ride the Flipping Fudge Pops Ferris Wheel."

Antonio and Tommy turned their faces to the ride.

"Unless," George said in a singsong voice, "you're too scared?"

"Who are you calling scared?" Antonio snapped. "My middle name is Danger!"

"I thought it was Harold," Tommy said.

Tommy stayed in line for their balloons. Antonio lagged a few feet behind the girls as they made their way to the Flipping Fudge Pops Ferris Wheel.

"Why are we going on a ride with Antonio?" Bess whispered.

"You'll see," George whispered back. "Just hold on to your pockets."

Nancy still didn't know what George had in mind, but she zipped the pocket that held her Clue Book. Bess snapped the pockets on her jackets too.

When all four kids were at the Flipping Fudge Pops gate, the attendant checked their heights. They were all tall enough to go on the ride.

A popsicle-shaped cage stood open. The Clue Crew and Antonio slipped inside. Two benches faced each other on opposite ends of the cage.

Nancy and Bess sat on one bench. George and Antonio sat on the other.

"Let's do this!" George declared.

"Yeah," Antonio growled. "Bring it!"

The door to the cage snapped shut. A bell rang. Steel safety bars lowered above the kids' laps.

"Woo-hoo!" Antonio cheered as their cage lifted off the ground. "This is going to be sick!"

"So am I!" Bess groaned as the cage began rocking back and forth. As the Ferris wheel turned, the cage rocked faster and faster—until it flipped all the way over!

Upside down, Antonio yelped. The stuff inside his pockets was spilling out all over the cage!

"Yes!" George cheered. "It worked! It worked!"

Chapter

TOWER OF SOUR

Nancy and Bess shrieked as Antonio's stuff rained all over them. The cage flipped back, and it all tumbled to the floor.

"Oh, no!" Antonio wailed.

When the ride came to a stop, Nancy's head was still spinning as she, Bess, and George looked at everything that had fallen. There was no candy-striped bracelet. Just a balled-up used tissue, a few crumpled dollar bills, a plastic toy magnifying glass, and lots of squirmy—

"Gummy Pests?" Nancy asked. "Was this the proof you were talking about?"

"Correct-o!" Antonio confirmed with a mischievous grin. "I dropped a gummy spider in Nadine's pocket when we were on the Sour Power Pals ride."

"Because Nadine got our fourth bracelet and not you?" Bess asked.

"Nah," Antonio said. "Because it was funny."

Nancy, Bess, and George weren't laughing.

The safety bars rose and the door swung open. Antonio scooped his stuff off the floor at once.

"You can keep the Gummy Pests," Antonio said as he left the cage. "They're on me."

"You mean they're on us," complained Bess as she pulled an icky gummy worm from her hair. "All over us!"

Nancy picked up something Antonio forgot. It was the plastic toy magnifying glass.

"I'll give it back to Antonio when we see him at school," Nancy decided. "Nobody should have to lose their stuff—even pests."

As they walked away from the ride, Nancy crossed off Antonio's name from her suspect list. "That leaves us with only one suspect."

"Or suspects," Bess said, sticking out her tongue. "Those Sour Power Pals!"

The Clue Crew made their way through Candy Kingdom toward the World of the Sour Power Pals. As they neared the ride, a booming voice made them jump: "Huzzah! Yonder roams our royal winners!"

Nancy, Bess, and George whirled around and smiled. It was the king and queen of Candy Kingdom!

"We see three of thee," the queen declared. "Where is Lady Gumdrop?"

"You mean Nadine?" Bess asked. "Oh, she went home because she lost—"

"She lost her lunch!" George cut in. "On one of the rides."

The king and queen blinked. "Oh."

Good save, Nancy thought. Nadine had asked the girls not to tell anyone about the missing bracelet. To change the subject she pointed to a small blue tower in the near distance. "Is that your castle?" Nancy asked.

The king shook his head. "Yonder stands the majestic Tower of Sour."

"Tower of Sour?" George repeated.

"It is for Sour Power Pals only!" the queen added.

Nancy, Bess, and George traded puzzled looks. A tower just for Sour Power? What was up with that?

"Alas, we must bid thee farewell," the king declared.

"We have a royal bubble-gum-blowing contest to judge," the queen told them.

Nancy, Bess, and George turned to examine the tower.

"Maybe the pals go there when they're not working on the ride," George suggested.

"Then that's where we're going next," Nancy stated. "To find clues and hopefully Nadine's missing bracelet."

Nancy, Bess, and George walked up to the blue tower. The walls looked like they were dusted with fake powdered sugar. Over the door was a sign that read KIDS OUT! THIS MEANS YOU!

"Even their sign is rude," Bess complained. "I don't think I want to go in there."

"Why, Bess?" George asked.

"What if the Sour Power Pals are inside right now?" Bess asked. "If they were mean on the ride, they'll be supermean when they find us snooping around."

The door also had a small round window. Nancy pointed up to it and said, "Let's peek through that window. If we see Sour Power Pals, we won't go inside."

The window was high. George was the highest jumper, so she jumped once, twice, three times to

reach it. But on the fourth jump, she landed hard against the door, pushing it wide open!

"Whoa!" George cried as she tumbled inside.

Nancy and Bess hurried in after her. They were standing in a small entrance hall; a winding staircase was straight ahead.

"Does anyone see Sour Power Pals?" Bess whispered.

"No," Nancy whispered. "But I do see their costumes."

Nancy pointed to three Sour Power Pals costumes, hanging from hooks on a wall. They were the same colors as the pals who had helped them into the boat—yellow, red, and blue.

"If the costumes have pockets," Nancy went on, "maybe Nadine's bracelet is in one."

"Pockets again?" Bess groaned. "After what we found in Antonio's, I'm afraid to look."

The Clue Crew headed straight to the hooks and the costumes. Each costume had a mask attached but no pockets.

If they did take Nadine's bracelet, Nancy wondered, *where would they put it?* Nancy's thoughts were interrupted by voices. They seemed to be coming from outside the door.

"It's got to be Sour Power Pals!" Bess squeaked. "They can't catch us snooping in here."

"Okay, we'll hide," Nancy said, looking around. "But where?"

"Up the stairs," George said. "Quick!"

The Clue Crew filed up the winding staircase. When they reached the top they received an unwelcome surprise.

Standing at the top of the stairs were the three pals—red, yellow, and blue. Nancy gulped as the pals stared icily at the girls. Things were about to get sour—and fast!

Chapter

ROBO-RIOT

"Um . . . we weren't snooping," Bess told the pals. "We were looking for the way out."

The three pals didn't move. They just stood silently and stared.

"We weren't looking for a way out," George said bravely. "We were looking for our friend's missing prize bracelet." Braver and braver, she stepped forward. "Well? Do you know where it is?"

The yellow pal finally blinked. Then—*WHIR,*

WHIR, WHIRRRRR! Its eyes glowed red and then flashed several times. The red pal's head whirled around and around on its neck. Out of the blue, the blue pal sang the Sour Power Pals song, repeating the same word over again: "Who needs sweet when you can have sour, sour, sour, sour, sour. . . ."

"They're not just mean," Bess cried. "They're out of control!"

"Let's get out of here," Nancy decided.

The girls turned to leave. They froze when they saw what was coming up the winding staircase—three more Sour Power Pals—red, yellow, and blue!

"News flash," George gulped. "We're surrounded."

The girls thought they were toast until one by one the Sour Power Pals pulled off their masks. Underneath were three teenage faces, two boys and a girl. They looked past Nancy, Bess, and George and sighed.

"Oh, great," one boy said.

"Here they go again," the girl said.

"Again?" George asked.

"Footsteps can activate them," the other boy explained, walking to the head-spinning pal. "It's happened before." He lifted a hidden panel on the pal's chest. After flipping a switch, the pal's whirling head came to a stop.

Switches were flipped on the other two pals. The singing and eye flashing stopped too. Soon all three Sour Power Pals stood silent and statue-still.

"No wonder these three were taken off the ride," the girl told the boys. "They've totally malfunctioned."

"You mean like robots?" Nancy asked.

"Here we call them animatronics," the girl explained.

"I like Robo-Pals better," George decided.

The teens introduced themselves. The girl was Bella. The boys were Jaden and Mike.

"And as you can see by our costumes," Jaden said, "we're also Sour Power Pals."

"You mean the ones from the ride?" Bess

asked. "You're too nice to be those creepy pals."

Jaden chuckled and said, "Thanks. I guess that means we're good actors."

"We have to act sour when we work on the ride," Bella explained, "or we wouldn't be Sour Power Pals."

"If you're so nice," George asked the pals, "why did our friend Nadine's prize bracelet go missing inside your ride?"

"Missing?" Bella repeated.

"I heard two Sour Power Pals talking," Nancy explained. "One said his friends would love a free week at Candy Kingdom."

"Who wouldn't?" Mike admitted with a grin. "But we would never steal anyone's prize bracelet."

"We wouldn't steal anything," Jaden added.

"Sour Power Pals may be sour on the outside," Bella said with a smile, "but we're totally sweet on the inside."

Nancy and Bess smiled too, but George wasn't convinced. She tilted her head as she studied the pals.

"Nobody was inside that ride," George said, "except us kids and you sweet-and-sour people!"

"You mean these guys," Jaden said, pointing to the Robo-Pals. "The only pals inside the ride are animatronics."

Nancy, Bess, and George stared at the teens and then at the Robo-Pals.

"You mean the pals blasting sugar and hurling marshmallows," Nancy asked, "are all robots?"

Suddenly—*WHIRRRRR!!! Boing! Boing!*

Bess shrieked as the blue Robo-Pal's eyes popped out straight at the girls.

"I'm outta here," Bess cried, before racing down the stairs.

"Thanks for your help, but we have to run!" Nancy told the pals. Then she winded down the twisty staircase after Bess. She could hear George's footsteps behind her.

At the bottom of the staircase, George turned to Nancy and Bess. "Why did we have to leave? I still think those sour suckers took Nadine's bracelet."

"But they were so nice," Bess argued.

"And I believed them when they said they would never steal Nadine's bracelet," Nancy added.

"I didn't mean the teenagers," George said. "I meant the Robo-Pals." She pointed up the staircase. "You saw how crazy they get when they're on the blink. Maybe crazy enough to steal a bracelet!"

Nancy had to admit that George knew a thing or two about gadgets, and that's what the Robo-Pals upstairs were—big out-of-control gadgets!

"Okay," Nancy said, "but how do we question robots?"

"We don't!" Bess declared. "Instead we leave this Tower of Sour now!"

Bess yanked a door open, but it wasn't the door leading outside. Instead, it led into a very small office. In it was a desk, a file cabinet, and a miniature model of the Sour Power Pals ride.

"Neat," George said. "Let's check it out!"

Nancy, Bess, and George gathered around the colorful mini model. It looked just like the real ride, only tiny.

"There are the boats on the lime-soda stream," Bess pointed out. "And the pink cotton-candy whirlpool."

"There are the Robo-Pals, too," George said, pointing at the model, "on those rock-candy mountains."

Nancy studied the model. Something about

the Robo-Pals and the boats stood out.

"Look how far the pals are from the stream," Nancy told Bess and George. "Their arms can't be long enough to reach the boats."

"Or Nadine's bracelet," Bess agreed.

George shrugged and said, "So I guess the Robo-Pals are clean."

"And the real Sour Power Pals," Bess said with a smile, "are not really mean!"

The Clue Crew found their way outside. As they walked away from the tower, Nancy crossed out the Sour Power Pals from her suspect list.

"That's it, you guys," Nancy said as she closed her Clue Book. "We have no more suspects. Zero. Zip. Zilch."

"What next?" George asked.

"Let's go back to the photo board," Bess said. "Now that I like the Sour Power Pals, I want to buy our picture."

The girls returned to the photo board. They found their picture in the exact same place.

"It is a good picture," Nancy said as they

looked it over again. "Even Nadine looks happy in it."

"No wonder Nadine was happy," Bess said. "She didn't know she lost her bracelet yet."

George tilted her head as she studied the picture.

"Then what's that thing around her wrist?" she asked.

Nancy studied Nadine in the picture. That's when her eyes popped wide open. It was a bracelet!

Chapter

THE BIG PICTURE

Bess looked at it too. "Is it a bracelet?" she asked. "Is it red and white and candy-striped? Can anyone tell?"

"I can't," George said, shaking her head. "The bracelet is way too small in the picture."

"Phooey," Bess said. "Too bad we don't have robotic magnifying eyes."

Nancy smiled to herself. She didn't have magnifying eyes, but she did have the next best thing. . . .

"Ta-da!" Nancy declared as she pulled out Antonio's magnifying glass. "This ought to do the trick."

Bess and George watched as Nancy positioned the small round glass over the picture. After moving it a few times over Nadine's arm, the bracelet popped into view.

"Boom!" George declared. "Red and white and candy stripes all around!"

"Who knew Antonio would save the day?" Bess said.

Nancy nodded and said, "This is a game changer. The picture was taken at the end of the ride, right before we all got out of the boat."

"So Nadine couldn't have lost it earlier in the ride," George added, "like she said she did."

"But Nadine showed us that she didn't have the bracelet after the ride," Bess remembered. "If she didn't lose it inside the ride, how did she lose it?"

"I don't know," Nancy admitted. "But maybe Nadine does."

Bess was about to buy the picture as a souvenir and a clue when someone called, "Hi, girls. Having fun?"

Nancy knew that voice anywhere. It was her dad!

"Hi, Daddy!" Nancy said as Mr. Drew walked over with a wave and a smile. "Where's Hannah?"

"Hannah decided to shop for dinner," Mr. Drew explained. He lifted his sleeve to show the guest bracelet. "She lent me this so I could join you at Candy Kingdom."

"Awesome, Daddy," Nancy said excitedly. "You're just in time to drive us to Nadine's house!"

"Nadine's house?" Mr. Drew asked with surprise.

"We can get back into Candy Kingdom later," Bess explained. "All we have to do is show our bracelets."

"Thanks, Mr. Drew!" George said.

Mr. Drew stared at the girls. "But I just got here," he told them. "And I couldn't wait to ride the Marshmallow Mix-Up."

Nancy giggled to herself. Her dad may have been a lawyer, but most of the time he acted just like a big kid.

"We're working on a case, Daddy," Nancy explained. "Nadine was wearing her candy-striped bracelet—"

"A case?" Mr. Drew interrupted. "Why didn't you tell me? To the car, Clue Crew!"

"Are you sure, Mr. Drew?" Bess asked.

"Sure, I'm sure," Mr. Drew said with a grin. "Who needs the Marshmallow Mix-Up when your mysteries are such a wild ride?"

Bess bought their picture from a snarky Sour Power Pal. Then Mr. Drew drove the girls straight to Nadine's house.

"Thanks, Daddy," Nancy said. "Can we walk home after we talk to Nadine?"

"Sure thing," Mr. Drew said out the window. "As long as you're—"

"Together!" Nancy, Bess, and George chorused.

All three girls had the same rule. They could

walk anywhere in the neighborhood as long as it was no more than five blocks and as long as they were together.

Mr. Drew drove away. The Clue Crew stood on the sidewalk facing Nadine's house.

"What do we ask Nadine when we see her?" Bess asked.

But they didn't get a chance to make a plan, because the front door opened when they got to the driveway. Nadine stepped outside wearing the same jacket she'd worn to Candy Kingdom.

"Hi, Nadine," Nancy called.

Nadine didn't wave back. Or smile. Instead her hand dropped down over her jacket pocket.

Nancy watched as Nadine's hand pressed against her pocket tightly. It was then that something clicked for Nancy. . . .

"Bess, George," Nancy murmured. "I think I know who took the bracelet."

Clue Crew—and YOU!

Now's your chance to think like the Clue Crew and solve the mystery of the missing candy-striped bracelet! Or turn the page to solve this whodunit.

1. So far the Clue Crew ruled out Andrea, Antonio, and the Sour Power Pals. Can you think of more bracelet-grabber suspects? Get a paper and pen and then write down your answers.

2. When Nadine covered her pocket, it gave Nancy an idea. Do you know what her idea might be? Write one or more on a piece of paper.

3. Antonio's lost magnifying glass came in handy for Nancy, Bess, and George. What other tools might be helpful for detectives like the Clue Crew—and you?

Chapter

10

WRIST TWIST

"Who, Nancy?" Bess whispered. "Who took Nadine's bracelet?"

"Nadine!" Nancy whispered back.

"Why would Nadine steal her own bracelet?" George hissed.

"You saw how upset Nadine was," Bess reminded her. "She was practically crying over her lost bracelet."

"Nadine's an actress, remember?" Nancy

whispered. "Anyway, we have to look inside her pocket right now."

"Another pocket?" Bess groaned. "Great."

"What are you guys talking about?" Nadine called as the girls walked up the path. "I have to run an errand for my mom."

"This won't take long, Nadine," Nancy said. "We just want to ask you something."

Nadine raised an eyebrow. "You do? What?"

"Here's our picture from the end of the Sour Power Pals ride," Bess explained as she held it up. "In it you're still wearing your candy-striped bracelet."

"Impossible," Nadine insisted, shaking her head. "I lost my bracelet somewhere inside the ride. I told you I felt some kind of tug, remember?"

"That must have been Antonio," George said coolly.

"Antonio?" Nadine asked surprised.

"Antonio Elefano was sitting right behind you on the boat," George explained. "He told us he dropped a spider in your pocket—"

"Spider?" Nadine cried. "Ewwwww!"

Nancy, Bess, and George watched as Nadine frantically emptied her pockets. Out flew a pack of gum, a cherry lip balm, a squiggly gummy spider, and last but not least a red-and-white candy-striped bracelet!

George looked at the bracelet and then pumped her fist. "My plan worked again," she declared. "I am on a roll!"

Nadine wasn't celebrating. "Phooey," she murmured under her breath. "I should have known the Clue Crew would figure it out."

Nancy picked up the red-and-white candy-striped bracelet. It was exactly like the ones she, Bess, and George were wearing. The missing bracelet!

"Why did you do it, Nadine?" Nancy asked gently. "Why did you take off your own bracelet and hide it from us?"

Nadine blinked away tears. She then threw back her shoulders and said, "Because I didn't want to ride the Twisting Taffy Coaster. That's why."

The Clue Crew stared wide-eyed at Nadine.

"The Twisting Taffy Coaster?" Nancy repeated. "Why didn't you want to ride it?"

"I'm scared of roller coasters," Nadine confessed. "More than I'm scared of icky spiders."

"The one in your pocket was a Gummy Pests candy," Bess said.

"It's still gross," Nadine sniffled.

Nancy, Bess, and George listened as Nadine explained everything: how she pulled off her bracelet while the girls were running toward the Twisting Taffy Coaster. How she stuck it in her jacket pocket and told them it was lost.

"I think I get it, Nadine," George said. "If you didn't have the bracelet, you couldn't go back to Candy Kingdom."

"And if you couldn't go back to Candy Kingdom," Bess added, "you wouldn't have to ride the Twisting Taffy Coaster."

"Right," Nadine murmured.

Nancy felt bad for Nadine and understood

why she hid her bracelet. But there was still something she didn't get.

"Why didn't you tell us, Nadine?" Nancy asked. "Why didn't you tell us you didn't want to ride any coasters?"

"Because you gave me your fourth prize bracelet!" Nadine exclaimed. "I didn't want to spoil your fun by being a downer!" She heaved a sigh and said, "Sorry. I don't blame you if you take someone else to Candy Kingdom this week."

"Someone else?" Nancy repeated. She smiled as she shook her head. "We want you to come with us to Candy Kingdom, Nadine."

Nadine gasped while Bess and George nodded in agreement. "Me?" she said. "Are you sure?"

"Totally," Bess declared. "And you don't have to ride the Twisting Taffy Coaster if you don't want to."

"You're not a downer either," George told Nadine with a smile. "A drama queen sometimes . . . but never a downer."

Drama queen? Nancy's eyes lit up as the words gave her an idea . . .

"Nadine?" Nancy asked. "Why don't you try acting like someone who's brave on coasters and loves them too?"

"Yeah, Nadine," Bess agreed. "If you act brave, maybe you'll feel brave too!"

Nadine finally smiled. "I played a squirrel one year in the class play," she said, "and I had a craving for nuts a whole week."

"So?" George asked.

"So," Nadine declared happily, "it might work!"

The next morning, Nancy's dad drove the Clue Crew and Nadine back to Candy Kingdom. Mr. Drew was happy to ride the Marshmallow Mix-Up. Nadine rode the Twisting Taffy Coaster, not once, but twice!

"You did it, Nadine!" Nancy cheered.

Nadine's candy-striped bracelet dangled around her wrist as she planted both hands on her hips.

"You mean Princess Extrema," Nadine announced. "Coaster Hero of the Universe!"

Nancy, Bess, and George exchanged smiles.

Their friend was back at Candy Kingdom and better than ever!

"And guess what, Nadine?" Nancy asked. "You can ride the Twisting Taffy Coaster every day this week."

"And the Bubble Gum Bobsled, the Gumdrop Go-Carts, the Licorice Loop-the-Loop, and Minty Matterhorn!" Bess said.

"There's only one word to describe all that," George said with two thumbs-up. "SWEET!"

Test your detective skills with another Clue Book mystery:

Nancy Drew Clue Book #8:
World Record Mystery

by CAROLYN KEENE · illustrated by PETER FRANCIS

"Go, Katie! Go, Katie!"

Nancy Drew and her best friends, Bess Marvin and George Fayne, joined the rest of the crowd cheering for River Height's teen Katie McCabe as she spun across the electronic floor pad of the Dance-A-Thon video game. The arcade was full of fans watching the gaming whiz practice her moves. Katie's feet flew fast on the lit-up squares, and she added arm movements to match the rhythm. In just a few hours, a judge from the

Beamish Book of World Records would be there to record Katie's attempt to break the current high score!

"This is so exciting!" exclaimed Nancy.

"I hope by the time I'm sixteen *I* can dance like Katie," Bess said. She tried out a kick step and almost crashed into George.

Nancy laughed. "Good thing you have a few years to practice. I think you might need them."

Nancy and her friends were eight, and even though they didn't have dance moves like Katie, they were already experts at one thing: solving mysteries. Nancy, Bess, and George called themselves the Clue Crew.

George shook her head, causing her short brown hair to flop this way and that. "I know dancing takes a lot of athletic skill, but I'll take soccer over sashaying anytime."

George was the tomboy of their group. She and her cousin Bess were as different as night and day, but that didn't stop them from being close as could be.

Bess pulled her blond hair into a ponytail and fastened it with a sparkly clip. "I just hope the judge hurries up and gets here."

Nancy laughed at her eager friend. "I hate to tell you, but I heard that the judge isn't scheduled to arrive for a couple of hours. That just means we have time to play some games of our own, if you want."

George led the way to the change machine that let them exchange their allowance money for game tokens. "How about some Skee-Ball to start?" she suggested. "It's my favorite."

The three girls took turns bowling at the Skee-Ball game. Bess got three balls into the tiny opening, worth one hundred points, and collected six tickets when the game ended.

"I'm saving up for the lava lamp I saw behind the prize counter," Bess said. "It will look super groovy in my room! And the base is pink—my favorite!"

"You'll need to win a lot more games to have enough tickets for a prize that big, Bess," Nancy said, handing her friend the three she'd scored.

"I have that same lava lamp in my arcade and it costs seventy-five fewer tickets than here."

The girls turned around to find Christopher Finn, the owner of Gamespot, just behind them. His arcade was down the street and was another popular hangout spot for the kids in River Heights.

"Sorry to eavesdrop," Mr. Finn said, stuffing his hands in his pockets. "It's just so crowded in here, I couldn't help but stand close."

Nancy was jostled again, this time by a kid racing past her to the photo booth. She grimaced. "That's okay, Mr. Finn. There *are* a ton of people in here today."

"Tell me about it," he replied. "My arcade's practically a ghost town this morning. Everyone would rather be here, cheering on Katie. I sure wish I had the Dance-A-Thon game at my place."

Mr. Finn hung his head and shuffled past the girls. Bess, Nancy, and George shared a sympathetic look, but it only took a few moments for them to get back in the mood to play.

The arcade was full of energy and sounds: bells, dings, chimes, laughter, and happy squeals!

Nancy was a pro with the giant padded hammer as she earned eight tickets at Whack-A-Worm. Next the girls climbed into plastic cars that moved them side to side and up and down as they raced one another on big screens in front of them. Bess and Nancy leaned into the racetrack turns while George yelled at her car to go "faster, faster!"

When they were done racing, Bess and George played against each other in air hockey. For two girls so different, their skills were well-matched and the game ended in a tie score.

"Hmm, I know we said I'd play the winner, but how will we pick now?" Nancy asked, rubbing her chin.

"I'll play you, Nancy."

The girls spun around to see Michael Malone holding up a game token in his hand. Michael was in fourth grade and a close buddy of Ned Nickerson, one of Nancy's friends.

"Sure, Michael. I'll play you," Nancy said. "Are you any good?"

Michael held the token up to the sky and blew on it, before dropping it into the air hockey machine and pressing Start.

"Not to brag too much, but I'm good at every game. I have the high score on three of the machines here."

He flipped the red puck in his hands before setting it onto the center of the table.

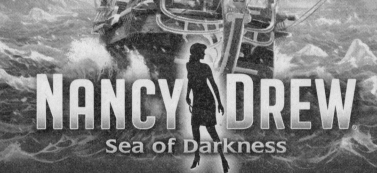

Looking for another great book?
Find it
IN THE MIDDLE.

Fun, fantastic books for kids
in the in-be**TWEEN** age.

IntheMiddleBooks.com

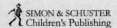